BILLY AND THE MONSTERS

Monsters at Halloween

ZANNA DAVIDSON

Illustrated by MELANIE WILLIAMSON

Meet Billy...

Billy was just
an ordinary boy
living an ordinary
life, until
ONE NIGHT
he found
five
MINI MONSTERS
in his sock drawer.

Gloop   Peep   Fang-Face   Captain Snott   Trumpet

Then he saved their lives, and they swore never to leave him.

We give you the Secret-Hairy-Snot-Tooth Oath of Devotion.

When he moved house, Billy found ANOTHER monster.

Hello. My name's Sparkle-Bogey.

One thing was certain – Billy's life would never be the same AGAIN...

Contents

Chapter 1
Monster Time

It was Halloween and Billy was showing his **SCARY** costume to the Mini Monsters.

> What do you think? I've even got a zombie hand.

"Tonight," said Billy, "we're going trick-or-treating around the village. You can all hide in my special Halloween bucket."

"And then," Billy went on, "we're going to a **SPOOKY PARTY!**"

"What's the matter?" asked Billy.
"I don't like Halloween," said Peep. "It's too scary."
"What are you scared of?"

"MONSTERS," whispered Peep.

But YOU'RE a monster!

I know. But only a very small one.

"Don't worry, Peep," said Billy. "You'll be fine. As long as everyone

stays
out of
trouble."

"We never cause any trouble," said Fang-Face.

Billy thought of all the times this week the Mini Monsters had got him into trouble.

At Auntie Nora's house...

Gloop getting into Auntie Nora's handbag.

At home...

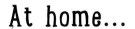

Fang-Face eating
my socks AGAIN.

At the park...

Fang-Face
chasing a dog.

Visiting
Grandma...

Trumpet parping in
front of Grandma
(so it looked like
it was me).

"Actually," said Captain Snott, "this is the best time for us to be out. People will be

EXPECTING

to see scary monsters."

"Not my mum!" said Billy, hearing footsteps. "Quick, everyone – HIDE! I think she's coming."

"Are you ready, Billy?" asked
his mum.

"*I'm* ready," said his sister, Ruby.

"Now, I want you two on your
BEST BEHAVIOUR tonight," said
their mum. "Everyone in the
village will be there."

"I'll be running the apple bobbing, with apples from our own garden," she added proudly. "And your dad is organizing **Guess the Body Part**."

I really feel as if we're starting to belong here.

Groan...

Mwa ha haaa! cackled

Billy's dad, coming up the stairs.

"**Gosh!**" said Billy's mum. "Do you think maybe you've gone too far?"

"Not at all," said Billy's dad. "I'm sure lots of other parents will be dressed up."

We're going to fit right in.

Chapter 2
Trick or Treat?

Hi, Billy!
Hi, Ruby!

Hello, Ash!

Everyone was gathered in the village square for trick-or-treating. Billy and Ruby couldn't wait to start filling up their buckets with sweets.

Oh. I think I'm the only grown-up in costume.

As the man started giving out sweets, Billy put down his bucket so his Mini Monsters wouldn't get squashed.

Then Billy held out his hands.

"Wow!" Billy said to Ruby.
"Look how many sweets I've got."

But when Billy looked for his
bucket, he couldn't find it
ANYWHERE.

In its place was a much paler bucket. "Oh no!" Billy realized.

"Someone's taken my BUCKET!"

Never mind. Can't you use this one instead?

But I really want MY bucket!

Billy turned to Ruby. "The Mini Monsters were INSIDE my bucket!" he whispered. "And now they've GONE!"

It's raining sweets! This is amazing.

Sweets taste better than ties.

But not as good as socks.

26

Take us to Billy at the Halloween Party!

VILLAGE HALL

It worked. We're at the party.

I LOVE parties.

It must be MAGIC.

Chapter 3
Maggoty Maggots

"This is terrible," said Billy, as he and Ruby went from house to house.

I keep looking at everyone's buckets but I can't tell which one is **MINE**.

"Never mind," said Billy's mum. "It's time for us to go to the **HALLOWEEN PARTY**. Please *try* to behave," she added. "I really want us to make a good impression."

As soon as they arrived at the
village hall, Billy's mum went over
to organize the apple bobbing.

Billy went to look for his bucket.

"What are you doing, Billy?" asked his friend Ash. "Let's try the apple bobbing."

"Er, okay," said Billy, trying to act normal.

But then, out of the corner of his eye, he spotted *Sparkle-Bogey* on the rim of the enormous tub!

"Hooray!" thought Billy. "The Mini Monsters aren't lost – they're AT the party!"

But then, as he watched, Sparkle-Bogey **WIBBLED**…

…and **WOBBLED**…

…and fell **FACE FIRST** into the water.

SPLISH!

The girl at the front of the queue stepped forward to try and catch an apple. IN HER MOUTH.

Billy LEAPED in front of the apples.

"What are you doing?" asked the girl. "I want to have my go."
"I saw something... in the water..." said Billy quickly.

Billy thought hard. What could be so bad that no one was allowed to do apple bobbing?

"Maggots!" cried Billy. "The apples are full of **MAGGOTS!**"

"**Urgh!**" screamed the girl, clamping her hands over her mouth. "I nearly **ATE A MAGGOT!**"

Everyone started backing away from the apple bobbing.

"There aren't any maggots in these apples!" said Billy's mum. "I checked them!"

But **no one** was listening.

In all the confusion, Billy plunged his hand into the water and pulled out *Sparkle-Bogey*.

Billy's mum began inspecting the apples. "I can't see any maggots!"

"Oh," said Billy. "I was **REALLY** sure I saw them. It must have been my... imagination."

"You're up to something, Billy," said his mum. "I can tell. Don't cause ANY MORE trouble!"

I'll TRY not to...

Five more to find...

40

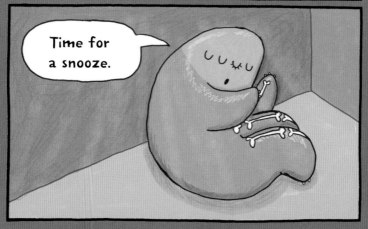

Chapter 4
Something Slimy

Billy took Sparkle-Bogey to a quiet corner of the hall. "Are you okay?" he asked.

Sparkle-Bogey nodded, and sneezed. "But I don't know where the others are," she said. "We all went in different directions to try and find you."

Then Billy felt a tap on his shoulder. Billy quickly put Sparkle-Bogey in his pocket and turned to see his friend, Ash.

Did you really see maggots?

I thought I did.

Ash laughed. "Maybe you just have a very good imagination. Come on. Let's go and play

GUESS THE BODY PART!"

Billy followed Ash across the
hall, his eyes searching for any
sign of the Mini Monsters.

They joined the queue to play "Guess the Body Part" and watched as a girl slid her hand into the box.

Come and play **"Guess the Body Part"!**

I can feel something **REALLY** slimy in here.

HOW TO PLAY
"GUESS THE BODY PART"
1. Put your hand in the box
2. Guess which body part you can feel!

"It can't be moving," said Billy's dad.

The girl
screamed. "It's
DEFINITELY
moving."

Aaarrrgh!

She snatched her hand away. "Are
you sure, sweetie?" asked her mum.
Then SHE put her hand in the box.

Aaaaarrrggghhh!

The mum snatched her hand away too. She looked like she might faint. "What is it?" she whispered. "What's in there?"

"Just food," said Billy's dad. "Spaghetti, peeled grapes…"

A group of kids was now crowding around the box.

Billy knew he had to act fast.
Any moment now, someone
was going to find Gloop.

"My turn!" he
announced, plunging his
hand inside the box.

Aaaaaaaaarrrrrrrgggggggghhh!

"What is it?" everyone cried.
"Something's BITING ME!"
said Billy.

He pulled out his **ZOMBIE** hand.

"Help! It's bitten off my hand!"

Ha ha, Billy! Very funny!

While everyone was looking at his zombie hand, Billy snuck his other hand back into the box and secretly pulled out Gloop.

Then he slipped Gloop into his pocket and moved away.

Look! There's nothing moving in here.

How odd. I was sure I felt something.

Hmm.

"Yikes," thought Billy. "That was close." He still had **four** Mini Monsters to find and people were definitely starting to get SUSPICIOUS...

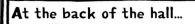
At the back of the hall...

Hooray!
I've found
CHEESE!

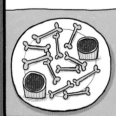

I just need
to find a safe
place to eat it.

54

Perfect!

You can't stay here.

Why not?

56

Don't worry!
I'll use my
magic wand.

It's not working!
It's **RUN OUT
OF MAGIC.**

Chapter 5
Squeaking Pumpkins

"I can't find all the Mini Monsters on my own," thought Billy. He looked around for Ruby and spotted her by the snack table.

"The monsters are at the **PARTY**," he whispered. "I've found Sparkle-Bogey and Gloop."

Can you help me find the others?

Ruby nodded.

"But we've got to be quiet about it," said Billy. "No one must notice that we're up to something."

Just then, they heard shouts behind them. A group of children had started carving the pumpkins.

This is fangtastic!

"That's odd," said one of the boys. "My pumpkin is making squeaking noises."

Billy and Ruby looked at each other. They were both thinking the same thing.

OH NO! There must be a Mini Monster INSIDE the pumpkin!

The other children stopped
carving and bent down to listen.

Then there was silence. "Let's see
if it does it again," said a little girl.
She picked up her pumpkin carver.

"DON'T touch that pumpkin!" shouted Ruby.

"Why not?" asked the girl.

Lots of people were gathered around the pumpkin table now – including Billy and Ruby's parents.

"But you don't have a pet rat," said her dad.

"I found one," said Ruby. "When we were trick-or-treating. I wanted to keep it as a pet, so I put it in that pumpkin."

Great plan, Ruby.

"You mean there's A RAT IN THAT PUMPKIN?" said the girl.

Ruby nodded.

Some of the parents had turned very white.

"I'll just take it outside and check it's okay," said Ruby.

Everyone watched Ruby go outside. Then they turned to Billy and his parents.

You're new here, aren't you?

Inside the bucket...

I hate Halloween.

I'm just going to wait here until Billy finds us.

I LOVE Halloween.

I'm not going anywhere until I've eaten **ALL THESE SWEETS.**

Only five more sweets to go.

Oh no! The skeleton boy's back.

68

Chapter 6

Best Party Ever!

At the back of the hall, a boy suddenly called out, **"HELP!** There's a **GHOST** in my bucket!"

"Uh oh!" thought Billy. He came running over and there was Peep, hovering in the air.

Billy caught hold of him.

What IS that thing?

It's my toy ghost.

"It's remote-controlled," explained Billy. "I must have pressed the 'fly' button by mistake. You see –

that's actually my bucket."

All the other kids were staring at Peep in the palm of Billy's hand.

"There's another one in the bucket," said Ash, who had come over to join them. "It looks like a tiny werewolf!"

"Er, unfortunately I have to go home now," said Billy, desperately looking around for his family.

Then he saw his mum and Ruby by the entrance. "Can we go now?" he whispered.

"I think that might be a good idea," said his mum. "I found Ruby outside. Luckily the rat seems to have run off."

I've got Sparkle-Bogey and Trumpet.

Hooray! We've got all the monsters.

"And there's your dad," his mum went on, beckoning him over.

"We're off now!" she said. "Sorry if we caused any trouble."

"It's been the best Halloween party ever!" said one of the girls.

Maggots in the apples!

A rat in a pumpkin!

Amazing toy monsters!

"Well, the children certainly
enjoyed it," said one of the mums.
"Do come again next year."

"Thank you," said Billy's dad,
beaming.

On the way home, Billy's dad
put his arms around everyone.
"Well that went very well," he
said. "I told you we'd fit right in."

"What about you, Peep?"
asked Billy.

Peep grinned. "I LOVE Halloween,"
he said. "I've found out I can be a
scary monster after all."

All about the MINI MONSTERS

CAPTAIN SNOTT →

LIKES EATING: bogeys.

SPECIAL SKILL:
can glow in the dark.

SCARE
FACTOR:
5/10

← GLOOP

LIKES EATING: cake.

SPECIAL SKILL:
very stre-e-e-e-tchy.
Gloop can also swallow his own
eyeballs and make them reappear
on any part of his body.

SCARE
FACTOR:
4/10

FANG-FACE →

LIKES EATING:
socks, school ties, paper, or
anything that comes his way.

SPECIAL SKILL:
has massive fangs.

SCARE
FACTOR:
9/10

TRUMPET →

LIKES EATING: cheese.

SPECIAL SKILL:
amazingly powerful
cheese-powered parps.

SCARE FACTOR:
7/10

(taking into
account his parps)

PEEP

LIKES EATING: very small flies.

SPECIAL SKILL: can fly (but
not very far, or very well).

SCARE FACTOR:
0/10 (unless you're afraid of
small hairy things)

SPARKLE-BOGEY →

LIKES EATING:
glitter and bogeys.

SPECIAL SKILL:
can shoot out
clouds of glitter.

SCARE FACTOR:
5/10 (if you're scared of
pink sparkly glitter)

Series editor: Becky Walker
Designed by Brenda Cole
Cover design by Hannah Cobley
Reading consultant: Alison Kelly

First published in 2019 by Usborne Publishing Ltd., Usborne House,
83-85 Saffron Hill, London EC1N 8RT, England. www.usborne.com
Copyright © 2019 Usborne Publishing Ltd. UKE

BILLY AND THE MINI MONSTERS
Monsters in the Dark

by ZANNA DAVIDSON Illustrated by MELANIE WILLIAMSON

BILLY AND THE MINI MONSTERS
Monsters on the Loose

by ZANNA DAVIDSON Illustrated by MELANIE WILLIAMSON

BILLY AND THE MINI MONSTERS
Monsters to the Rescue

by ZANNA DAVIDSON Illustrated by MELANIE WILLIAMSON

BILLY AND THE MINI MONSTERS
Monsters on a Plane

by ZANNA DAVIDSON Illustrated by MELANIE WILLIAMSON

BILLY AND THE MINI MONSTERS
Monsters at a Party!

by ZANNA DAVIDSON Illustrated by MELANIE WILLIAMSON